T0090447

Seasons of Faith

by annie richards

Trafford
PUBLISHING www.trafford.com
North America & international
toll-free: 1 888 232 4444 (USA & Canada)
fax: 812 355 4082

Table of Contents

Acknowledgement

A huge "Thank You" to so many of my friends, especially Gwen who gave me the encouragement to produce this product. A special recognition to my husband, whose love and support throughout these many years, not only encouraged me, but was my sounding board and computer expert.

Foreword

(A Muse)

I write because I cannot contain these thoughts within me. I write in the quiet of the moment, in the stillness of the night, because it is at those times I feel no boundaries. I am free to ponder the deepest joys, and yes, the harshest griefs. It is in those hours I experience blessings far above my greatest expectations. It is in those hours, when one can humble themselves, that it is no longer they that live, but the Spirit which lives within us.

In penning these thoughts, I am able to gain more understanding, wisdom, compassion and insight into this world of mine. I am able to examine the sensibilities and acumen of myself as well as others. Once committed to paper, one can perceive more objectively what their stand in life is and the interrelationship to others.

Were I to verbalize, would position myself for retort, thereby creating the dilemma of a response, perhaps clothed in apprehension, guarded so as not to seem foolish. Truly, in verbalizing ones' thoughts, there must be a listener, and the words which reach the listeners ears can be interpreted as to how that person feels at that moment, what circumstances are involved and the relationship from one to the other.

Writing, or penning as I prefer to call it, can be picked up and put down many times. The words are always there, only changing in the mind of the reader. This can conceivably allow them the freedom to decline, accept, understand or enlighten.

So come away with me and experience the freedom of the Muse. Let that unconstraint take you to the topmost heights or deepest depths. Whichever, however or whatever you do, your senses will be alive. Your kinship with nature, your Creator, your most inner self, will be revealed. This is life, and being life, allows you to understand the living.

Contemplation

Despite the yearnings
of the heart,
so often when we seek
to care
we feel so far apart.

What does it mean
to contemplate
the fluid of emotions

The masks we wear
the thoughts not shared
would swell the seas and oceans.

What does it mean
to meditate
our universal problems

of war, peace, hate, love
the deepest depths
the heights above

This pageantry of life
goes on and on
begetting times both kind and mean

Wherein many a tear
lies in the heart
and therefore, never seen.

Assurance

It's through our tribulations
strength will arise.
Although our trials beset us
patience is developing.

Should we find ourselves despairing
hope is being honed.
Through the daily strife of life
love is perfected.

If someone is disloyal to you
forgiveness is created
Thereby, such is the honorable
character developed.

Without these sensitive dispositions
which make us who we are,
life and life's' relationships
would hold no value.

A Child of Love and Laughter

I dream I was a child
of love and laughter,
not one who feels
hurting ways and deeds.

Years of isolation
years of timidity
years of dreaming dreams
without profanity.

One, who throughout
their childhood life
misses blocks of time....

Yet experiences
the one who yields
endless scars of crime.

Crying out
for that special love
only a mother can give.

Crying out
for that special past
to somehow identify with.

Living daily with
a lack of threat,
a life of wonder
awe – respect

A life of giving
a life of delight,
being special
in someone's eyes

Oh yes.............
I wish I was a child of
Love and Laughter

A Child of Love and Laughter

(A Short Story)

B..u...rrr...., tried as I might, I couldn't control the chatter of my teeth. It was a cold winter's morning. As I looked out of my window, billowy clouds were forming in the dark sky. They seemed alive and oblivious to the dawn, ready to unleash their contents on mother earth below. I had a chill. Our room, that is my sisters and mine, was always cold as it is in late December. I prayed Jess hadn't let the embers die out in the night. He, being the eldest, had to be sure there were enough coals to start a fire in the morning. If not, the day would start out something awful. The three of us older kids would be in for a licking that would never stop. Those embers dying out meant not only a cold room, but a cold and foreboding house. Grouchy angry people, hurt feelings and hurt bodies, and to crown it all no breakfast for at least two to three hours until things warmed up!

Jess fourteen, was the eldest of the six of us kids, my sister Leah being four years younger, then me, two years later. Actually, there were the three of us from my Dad and Mom. Mom died giving birth to me. The other three kids were Dad and Margaret's; *we were made to call her Mom.* Benji, was their eldest at seven, Doreen at five, followed by little Will, who was one. You would have to say this was a "pacel" of kids. I felt a lot of things about Jess. He was fun to be around. He could build anything you wanted. A tree house, dog house, make rooms with the empty crates we had in the back yard, and one of the best Crawdad fishers in the county. He was a young lanky kid, quick witted, intelligent and always eager to please. Yet he was somber in so many ways. Margaret always seemed to instigate enmity between father and son, and that was something I thought about often. *Could it have been the love shared with another woman who brought Jess into this world?* I really couldn't figure it out. Jess loved the outdoors. I'd watch him play and think, *he runs with the wind*. He had a lot of love to give and would give it gladly, but it just didn't seem to be enough. That was as far as Margaret was concerned. Something about Jess just seemed to rile her. She'd put Dad into the mood of punishing Jess mercilessly. With each landing blow, I could feel my heart actually rip away. Why Dad didn't see this, I don't know. Guess it was that perfection again. He wanted all us kids to be perfect, when it wasn't so, frustration became anger and anger became abuse.

It wasn't that Dad was such a mean person all the time. Heck, I remember lots of good times, like last night. It's just that his temper would get the best of him. It was then all hell would break loose. An educated man, intent on having his own contracting business one day, he expected nothing less from each of us. Seen as a pillar in the community, well thought of as a stern disciplinarian, but loving father. He was a particular man, wanting just about everything in perfect order at all times. When it wasn't such, he'd "blow". An example of this would be when we would dust our house. Coming home in a bad mood, he'd take a clean white handkerchief and run it over the tops of the doors. Finding any wee amount of dust on the cloth, he'd work himself into frenzy. This could only be quelled when he was exhausted of beating. I can remember him saying that if he said "black is white", the Lord Almighty himself, couldn't say different. Whenever things didn't go well at work, he'd come home in that foul mood of his ready for a fight. I could tell his mood just the way he slammed the door to his truck and walked in the house. That's when my heart would start pounding, my stomach feel sick and I'd be scared as a mouse cornered by an old tomcat. I'd start stuttering or trembling. Didn't matter which, trembling would cause me to drop and break anything in my hands, *as a matter of fact; they called me dropsy during this period of time.* Stuttering would just increase his already agitated state. Either way was enough to bring down his wrath.

Margaret wasn't immune to this treatment either. One particular episode, which by the way wasn't unusual, was when Dad came home in a bitter mood. Why and how it started, I'll never know. What followed, I did. He beat her, then having taken all her clothes off shoved her out of the house for the night. There was this ditch behind the house in which she hid. That night, when everyone was asleep, Leah woke me up and told me to come with her. We were to crawl out of our bedroom window and take Margaret a blanket so she could keep warm. *This was so much like my Sis, she was always trying to mediate.* I was so darn scared of being caught. Dad had warned us that evening if we were to attempt to help Margaret, we'd get the same treatment. So there the three of us were, huddled in a blanket until the sun came up. Leah and I then quickly returned to our beds with the blanket before Dad got up. We knew, if caught, her bruises would match ours. Sometimes I think Margaret would aim Dad's vile temper towards us in an effort to protect herself. One night while returning from the bathroom and passing their bedroom, I can remember overhearing her tell Dad that the three of us kids were almost too much for her to handle. She said, she could not deal with sassy kids, especially Jess who disobeyed continuously. Of course I knew this not to be the truth. *Why she never left was a puzzle to me. She seemed pretty enough and mean enough in her quiet way to exist just fine. I sensed and hated her fake "put-on" towards us when others were around.* With that, Dad got up, marched into our rooms, called the three of us out. What started as a severe tongue lashing, ended up in an exhaustive physical beating. I can't remember this being done with Benji, Doreen or Will. Sure made me want to curl up and sleep away the pain of all this cyclonic madness.

Now Leah, that was something else. For some reason, at least beyond my comprehension, she and Margaret never quite got along. Leah was beautiful, talented and smart. She was outgoing and always loved the limelight. She would put on singing and dancing shows for the neighbors. Most times, a little bossy, but a doer and able to make life exciting. I'd notice many a time Margaret's back would stiffen when Dad's eyes would sparkle at Leah's doings. She was naturally gregarious. There were times Dad would be a bit cross and in Leah's bubbly way, she would have him smiling at her with seemingly pride. She seemed to reach out to him and he to her. It was during such changes in him, that I saw Margaret's face. She too, was smiling, but it was a smile which seemed taut and piqued. Margaret had the same reaction when I'd call Dad, "Daddy". The enmity, although masked was nevertheless there and not hidden from my eyes. To my way of thinking, Leah would have been the apple of Dad's eyes, had it not been for Margaret. Leah was the apple of my eyes, and I was just a kid. There wasn't anything she couldn't or wouldn't do, and her love of life couldn't be quelled, no matter how many beatings or berating she took. These episodes seemed to relentlessly occur without provocation. It was amazing to me to see how she would come back, stand tall and think positive about life. Following times like this, we would go into our bedroom alone, her almost hazel eyes, like Dad's at times, would say mounds and mounds to me no matter what her words were. It was these times that again, my heart would tear, slowly, surely, inevitably. I knew as she did that the physical pain would pass, but I wondered many times, was her heart being torn in two, as well? We never spoke on this level.

There seemed to be a quiet proud inner defiance in both Jesse and Leah. Something I quietly admired and identified as lacking in me. They would not yield nor bend when they knew they were right. Me, I capitulated, just so the peace was maintained. I did not know it then, but years later, they would be the ones to capitulate to these adults, I would quietly defy.

As I grew older, I was always amazed at the acute sensitivity that was within me. My memories as an infant to five years of age are somewhat fuzzy. I do recall having been with my paternal grandparents. After mother died, because I was a sickly infant, I was given in their care until I was stronger. Leah and Jess remained with my Dad. The recollections of spending so many hours with my Grandma were wonderful. The sweet scent of Gardenia Dusting Talc and Sen-Sen, the cuddling up within her soft arms, listening to her singing and storytelling, still brings warm thoughts of those days. It was at these moments I felt most beloved and special. I remember my grandparent's sternness as well, which was meted out with love and restraint.

Grandmother had pictures of Margaret and Dad on the piano. She would tell me that one day they would come to have me live with them, Jess and Leah. She would talk about how that would be such a happy time for me. She would tell me to be a good girl for them as I was to her. She would tell me to love my Dad as well as my sister and brother and new mother. All I knew is that in those moments, what I wanted to do is just change the subject and talk about our lives. For some reason, she seemed to need to reassure me that all would be wonderful and OK. I sensed this, but she was bent on reminding me, *as she would point to the pictures on the piano,* of what a wonderful day that would be. That day came,

Grandma had been preparing me for this departure for so long it seemed. She had bought me a pair of black patent leather shoes, a white dress with pink rosebuds on the bodice and white socks with pink lace around the tops. When grandpa came home from work, he saw me, picked me up high and told me I was a sweet rascal to love. We laughed and sang. Grandpa's deep rich voice and grandma playing the piano, how I loved these times, encouraged to sing along, as it was a prayer to God.

The hours went by so fast that morning. Margaret and Dad arrived; Jess and Leah were with them. All of a sudden I felt so much apprehension, I started to cry. At that, Grandma picked me up and said everything would be all right. Dad was wearing a brown suit and hat. Margaret had on a brown suit with a pale pink blouse. She had a cameo pinned to the side. Her hair was in an upsweep. She was very pretty to look at, as was my father handsome.

The prettiness stopped short though, as she embraced me and told me how pretty I looked. As this physical act was introduced an awakening of foreboding deep within me welled up. Fright became real, for I strongly sensed the mawkishness which I was to experience so many times in the future. That fake pronounced act of caring and trust. The profoundness of that one action, one small hug, was to shape my path with this family, present, and future.

I was forced wailing from my Grandmother's arms, into their car. Both Jess and Leah whispered for me to stop. I was inconsolable. A few minutes later, the car stopped at the side of the road.

My anticipation of going back to my Grandparents was pure joy. What happened next was to be forever indelibly set in my heart and mind. The door opened and my father dragged me out of the car and slapped me so forcefully across the face, I was stunned. With an admonishment of, "shut up or you'll get more", I was placed back in the car between Jess and Leah, thoroughly and completely frightened at this new existence.

I was or seemed to be an anomaly to both parents. I was quiet, shy, scared of my shadow, and the butt of many jokes from adults and cousins alike. They never seemed to know what to do with me. A hard working mindful child, yet an equal recipient of the senseless abuse, emotionally and physically. I was known to be a daydreamer. However my fantasies carried me off to lands which had fields of flowers, rainbows, love and laughter. The penance for these escapes was to be thought of as a timid mousey person, and one who cowers. *It was during this period, they would call me Mousey, mousey.* I certainly was not considered a doer. In any event, to my mind, it was worth it. How I loved to feel the serenity and peace as I found myself amid those flowers, the bluest of skies with billowy white clouds, as the suns radiance reached out to hold me in its' bosom, protected, snug and safe. These fantasies sustained me and gave me hope.

Benji, Doreen and Will seemed oblivious to all of this. Of course Will was just a baby, Doreen having recovered from a case of meningitis was doted on. Benji, well he was just Benji, cute, a pill sometimes but nevertheless, cute. All of us kids got along well and there were never any real hostile feelings among us. I especially loved my little brother Will. I would get him up in the middle of the night so Margaret could feed him, and then rock him to sleep after changing his diaper. Our daily chores were handed out according to ability. What one couldn't do, two could do better. We all pitched in with the older kids responsible for the younger. Our holidays were pretty great as a rule and tempers seemed to mellow during these celebrations.

As I huddled there in my bed, I remembered the previous nights' festivities which brought a smile to my lips. Dad and Mom were in a particularly good mood. Scurrying about, we had made room for the most beautiful pine tree in the lot. Dad had gone out and chopped it himself. He said you didn't call it a Christmas tree until it was fully decorated. He then brought out all the magical boxes with all our trimmings, adding newer ones made this year. The stringing of popcorn, eating half of it too, and cranberries, drinking warm cocoa and singing Christmas Carols – what excitement! Oh, how I prayed the embers hadn't died out.

I was immediately comforted as I could hear the crackling of wood. Jumping out of bed, I anticipated the sight which would greet me this morning. Sure enough, snuggled in the corner of the room was the most beautiful decorated pine tree in the world. I loved the hues of red, green, blue and gold, with silver strands shimmering down from its' branches. The presents underneath, wrapped with bright colorful paper and tied together with bows of red and green, holding treasures yet to be seen on Christmas morning. The sweet pungent scent of cinnamon throughout the house, to a ten year old, this had to be magic.

As I warmed myself by the old woodstove, I could think of nowhere else I would rather be. The milling and jabbering of my siblings in the background had yet to dispel my quiet reveries of what was to come in a few short days. *"Would my sisters like the tinker boxes I made them? Would my brothers like the clay pots, would baby Will play with his stuffed sock doll? What would I be getting?"* There were so many presents under that tree!

It was said, "It's the season to be giving", but to me, it was the season to be living; where life itself meant new regeneration of the senses, when all was good, merry, loving and kind. Savoring the deep reaches of oneself. It was an intimate awareness of growth and promise between Creator and Created, which fomented warmth in my soul. As I sat there mesmerized with what I saw, felt, what I smelled and touched, I knew that reality was but a fragment of time away. Any moment would bring me back into the hubbub of this world. This family, my family.

My reverie was broken for I heard my sisters' voice. *For now, my thoughts are put aside, but only for now.* The six of us children were practicing for our annual Christmas play of Jesus' birth. I was to be a shepherd. Of course Leah had it all together, who does what and who goes where. We would present this play to Dad, Margaret, Grandpa and Grandma, (her folks) early Christmas morning. This year Uncle Bill, Aunt Joe, and their four kids would be here. You would think they were of some importance the way Leah carried on. Reminding us we were having a real audience this year, we had to be really good.

Sis handed out the roles to everyone. I really didn't want to be a shepherd, girls are not supposed to be shepherds! I wanted to play Mary's part. However as Sis explained, she always played the part of Mary, for it was made for older girls. I shrugged and condescended as I almost always did with her. Will was to be Baby Jesus. As I went to get him as instructed, I felt his baby softness and knew he would make a perfect Baby Jesus. Even Jess was taking part as a king, and that was some doing on my sisters' part.

The morning went by, rehearsing and rehearsing, at times of course, interrupted by our standard chores of bed making, cutting wood, sweeping, dusting, and general housekeeping. Nevertheless, Sis a master of turning out great plays managed to give us the enthusiasm to participate and practice.

The morning slides into the afternoon when we're finally through practicing. Excitement is in the air; the folks are in a good mood and allowed us to go outside to play. It snowed last night. Snow balls, snowman, snow fights, and laughter, the thrill of looking skyward, closing my eyes, and then feeling the cold soft wet flakes land on my tongue and face, only to instantly melt. We are surrounded by light, white mounds of snow. With abandonment and glee we throw ourselves into the fluffy drifts. We double up with laughter as Benji slides into a drift so large he is almost totally covered. Alas, ruddy cheeks and frozen fingers declare it's time to go in. A dinner of golden chicken broth with dumplings and crisp apple salad prepares us for the evening radio shows,

It's now dark outside, and as my siblings sit around the radio listening to "The Green Hornet", the woodstove crackles and the Christmas tree with all its' colors, shimmers and sparkles in the corner. Again, I am taken with the warmth and smells of the room. Once more savoring the senses, feel, touch, smell, sights, and yes my blessings too, those of my Creator and his creations. At this moment, at this time, in this place, I have a sense of living, happiness fills my soul. Is this the life of love and laughter?

Abandonment

Thank you Lord – for taking us as we are
blemished and weak – Your always there.
Encouraging – loving – admonishing
always showing how much you care.

You are ever with us
as we do our daily mundane tasks
ready – willing to guide and support
whenever we need to ask.

In the heights of our joy
or in our darkest hour
You speak to us gently
and we experience your loving power.

You are with us
As we scale the highest peaks
to touch the grandeur of your works
for it's your beauty we long to seek.

You are with us in our quiet hours
as you are in the bustling of our day.
You are always ready to respond
if you feel we're being led astray.

Our Lord, Our God, what comfort we get
what joy, balance and self-control
to know You are there
So deep within our soul.

You inspire – You guide
your love is so true
our lives would be worthless
were it not for you.

So let us meet You ….. one by one
knowing you are Christ, our Redeemer
Gods only Son.

Who through his love
the Father meets his goal
of our obedience and love
we become once again – whole.

Confidence

I was but an infant, left desolate and ill
my Lord picked up the shattered pieces
and my heart knew.

I became a young child, alone in this land
searching for refuge where none could be found.
My Lord held me with his love,
and my heart rose.

Then, as a teen, owing to no one,
full of mischief and delight
questions to be answered, who – what – how
my Lord never left me
and my heart grew.

I then became a young adult,
fulfilling hopes and dreams
so very many indiscretions and self-denial,
Yet, my Lord protected me
and my heart swelled.

Now in the twilight of my life,
a time to meditate, reflect and see
just how blessed I've been and am,
that my Lord is still with me

The Battle

We go along life's highway
fully impressed with ourselves
too busy to "smell the roses"
Too busy to give Thanks for health.

Then... as we know it
life throws us a curve
we're caught up in illness...not rare
finding we're weak and vulnerable,
willing to give up ...if we dare.

Will we give up the fight
relinquish to pain that part
which is stoic and true,
short-circuit our senses, doubt our Creator
accept that which is easier to do?

Or does this battle bring a change in our life
not of pain or disease do I speak,
but the change that comes
from knowing ones' soul,
where it stands, is it strong, is it weak.

An awareness then looms of that part which is hurt
the bodily pain and distress
the questioning, why are we here at all
how do we reach our life's' quest
or what in life that quest truly is.

What have we done to deserve
so mortal a blow, a significant show
of our limited nature within.

It is then that our senses begin to transform
from ourselves to Him above
For our comfort, peace, and yes, our trust
and the assurance He gives of his love.

So smile my friend and be joyful with hope
not due to great deeds or tasks,
but only because He loves us so
We need only.....only to ask.

Living

It takes but a breath of life to exist
but to live takes much much more
a song, a look, a touch, a feel
something sensed, something real
ecstasy, pain, work, play
a promise of the coming day.

Each hour, each minute – such precious time
loving, sharing, planning, dreaming,
integrating hopes that are yours, mine.

To live, truly live, life must be shared
with a goal, a dream, with someone who cares
for to give of yourself unencumbered and true
is to know who you are, in all that you do.

This applies to you and applies to me
that wherever we are in this land,
we must always trust the Lord, our God
in obeying - His commands.

Living or existing is yours to choose
through your actions or by thought
however remember, the choice you make
is the life you will have wrought.

Compromise

A harsh rejection of our Lord
" Oh no, Never", we would say
lest we feel we're never wrong,
we praise Him every day.

A violent act toward mortality
never would we do such deed,
however, be unkind or seek revenge,
tastes so very sweet.

Judge a person right or wrong
"No, that's for the Lord to do"
yet, "I'm morally right and good",
could this be my point of view?

That we are mostly in the right
and others need be wise
our plates are full, we do our best,
we always compromise.

Awake – awake - and become aware
of thy errant ways within
for it's all the many sum of these
that perpetuate the sin.

Compromising has its' place
but not where the Lord is concerned,
for He will seal your compromise,
the day that he returns.

A Poets Thoughts

(A Muse)

How interesting it is to note that in all humanly endeavors we search and we ponder the things we value. We seek to create definitions and identity as to who we are and what we're about. This can be perceived as communication, and we strive for it as if it were a composite mass.

Communication is an art, just as surely as a great painting, a concerto, an ode, or a sculpture is art. Think, why is a sculpture great, a painting adored, or a concerto enjoyed? It is not because it is of itself, for if it were, would mean the same to all. It therefore is a transposition of thought, albeit in a specific genre according to ones' talent, and to be interpreted in relation to ones' experiences.

It is a transposition of thought, a thought the thinker or creator gives of himself to others. The "others" then, perceive this thought as their own. An example of this is the poet. The poet is one who transcends the material and comes in contact or communication with the purity of the thought or life substance itself. It is the expression of the thought that allows freedom of the listener to interpret as his own, their understanding.

It is not the painting, ode, etc, which defines its' own entity, nor is it the majestic towering of Redwoods, mountain peaks, nor the vitalism of the relentless surf pondering on its' shores. It is that of a purifying awareness and wonder of the genetic greatness of those creations. The poet who perceives this, must do so in terms of it's' genesis so that the purity extends itself out to the material, rather than succumbing from the material to the genesis.

We are metamorphasized when we "Let go – Let God". We become a new creation, our intellect deriving its' nourishment from the soul. It's then, the discernment of good and evil transposes itself into action. The thought becomes what is seen, touched and felt. The poet gives vision to this thought and the recipient receives it as his own. It is then and only then, that our lives are ever more open and able to enjoy and participate in this miracle of nature.

It is remarkable to me that nothing in this life is new, but rather lies there to be refined, a refinement since the beginnings of man. A process so artfully designed by our Creator, as to tempt us to claim its' originality.

We speak of the great works of men such as the Monet's, Socrates, Emerson's, Tchaikovsky's, but are not these works trans-positions of someone's 'thoughts, which we immediately recognize as plausible and physical? That recognition substantiating the innate purity of it's' genesis that is inherent and claimable in all mankind. Yet for the masses, it is hidden under self perceptions of those realities around us. Those things we can touch and see and readily define. In doing so we shortcut our potential for perfection. Are we not created in His image, that image of knowing both good and evil, having the empowerment of saintly perfection to choose by free will, the direction in our lives?

Therein the thought transcends the realities. The realities then become the actions of the thought. It is then those very actions become outward radiations to others of the goodness of life or into itself for worth and definition through self- grandiosity.

Lest the purity be lost in the process of the touch and see philosophy, the "I have" and "I did", creates an introspective personality that benefits the "I"; thereby disengaging oneself from the perfection of our Creator. Losing the "self" to the "our" addresses the triunes of our spirituality via the expression of thought in its' truest form. The poet, the artist, the composer, etc, is then sharing, not opining, as to what he is feeling. The receiver then takes this and interprets as his own, according to his own life experiences.

29

Point of No Return

There comes a time – if you're lucky,
you've fulfilled your many dreams,
scaled peaks, trod through valleys,
built relationships, worked out schemes.

You've met the ravished,
the mighty too
toiled daily, lived with gusto,
savored life, both old and new.

Many times you'll miss your mark
in trying to attain your goals,
nevertheless, you've persevered,
reaching out to life, taking hold.

How much of your life have you shared with others,
how much have you given, not got
has your life, as you've lived it, played a meaningful role,
or has it all been for naught.

No begrudging, no sad song,
but a stable peace within
a marvel of what this life has meant,
a sharing of joys for Him.

A time to be at peace with yourself,
triumphs and trials alike
a time to appreciate day after day,
gaining new depths and insights.

For whether it's by chance or by design,
you're at the life's' road you've earned
where there is more past then future left,
the Point of No Return

Holy Spirit

We have been given freedom
freedom to reach the skies,
not freedom to do wrong
but right, throughout
our mortal lives.

Yet we inherently love to do
the many wrongful things
and the good and true we fight
but when the Holy Spirit
produces its' fruit
it's then we're engulfed in The Light

Having love, joy, patience, peace
being gentle, good and kind
sharing in each others' troubles and needs
unbinding our souls and minds.

Faithfully fulfilling our role in life
wherever we are in this land
always knowing our purpose here
is to obey our Lords' commands.

The Busy Shepherd

Do you know me
lest you feel you do
what will you say of me
on the day of my demise?

What thoughts would you know
of my life, my person
my struggles, hopes and dreams?

For you elect to be my shepherd
and I am of your flock
or is the gathering of this flock
a simple numbers count.

Do you know your sheep, person to person
or are there so many, that one lays
wasted within their numbers?

I am the shepherd, you say
seek me and you shall find.
Night comes and we shall rest,
gather around me for comfort.

Gather around and I shall direct
Seek me for I am at Gods' work
and I will show the way.

I sought, I came, I yearned
but alas, lost was I in the
midst of the flock.

Search me out, comfort me,
feed me the Word to stay my doubts
teach me – love me......

What will you say at my demise
what will you say?

Obstructions

(A Muse)

It was early morning; I was sitting in my usual place, warm and comfy. As I looked at the window I could see the sun was beginning to rise for the day. I could see the sun, but not its' fullness, as it was being viewed through tinted windows, half-drawn mini-blinds and drapery sheers. Even so, I could tell it was bright enough to have me squint my eyes. At that moment, I wanted to get up, remove the curtains and blinds so I could see with more clarity this beautiful sunrise.

Sitting there on my sofa, cuddled in a warm blanket, reading Scripture was just too comfortable for me to move. The sun was still shining, and I knew it would soon lose its' rising effect. I was torn between getting up from my place of comfort and seeking more clarity of this panorama.

I soon began to notice the sun losing its' intensity effect. At that awareness, I jumped up out of my comfort zone and rushed to the window to pull away the curtains and blinds which were obstructing the clarity of my view. I was too late! The sun had passed its' intense brilliance and I was not able to see all that it really offered.

I have to ask myself, how many times have I cheated myself out of experiences that would enrich my life? How many times have I missed the joy of seeing nature as it was created? How many times, remaining in my comfort zone, have I failed to be a part of this changing world? Am I really a part of the sights, the smells, the feels?

Is my relationship with my Lord like that – how many "curtains of obstruction" do I have in my life. These "curtains of obstruction" which are in themselves innocent, yet keep me from the full benefits my Savior has to give?

I felt bereft, I wanted to cry, there was something deep down in my very core that was affected by this experience. Was my Jesus honing me once again, for his purpose? In this I take refuge, I will seek out those innocent "curtains of obstruction" in my life. It is then that I may be able to experience the fullness of his promises, the richness of his love and the sureness of my destiny,

Lifes' Onus

We stumble along life's' highway,
striving to perfect our ways
endearing our hearts to others,
with deeds, talk and praise.

There are those who speak
of, it's me, it's mine, I am
justifying their daily deeds
in the wants and cares of man.

Never questioning a lack thereof,
or why we're created so grand
ever intense in our desires to seek
our place, neglecting the Masters' plan.

For having been created,
and not a product of our past,
but an offspring of our future,
to create a love that lasts.

A love lasting through generations,
yours, mine, theirs, ours
enabling others by serving,
thereby giving them power.

Then, as time continues to pass
and we are thought of in past tense,
we will have served as brothers and sisters in Christ
a life which had purpose and sense.

Standing Firm

Faith adds goodness and balance to life
perseverance, kindness and love,
discernment of the seductions at bay
comes with strength from above.

Taking a stance, strong and bold,
in the knowledge of Christ, our Lord
adds assurance and joy to our lives,
as the prophets past foretold.

For prophecy near had its' origins in man,
but tis man fulfilling these deeds
as the Spirit exists and reigns in him,
thwarting the threat within.

And so we mark our time here on earth
serving through His Word
eager to do our Masters work,
willingly and assured.

That in the end, blameless and true,
spotless and at peace
we've met the challenge with wisdom and grace
to reach our apotheosis.

Him

He always leads me
He always leads me
He always leads me, everywhere I go

He always feeds me
He always feeds me
He always feeds me, nourishing my soul.

In the twilight of the evening or middle of the day
in the soundest of my slumber He's always with me
So that far I'll never stray.

Maxims By Choice

How is it that, "Time stands still"
yet passes in swift flight?
How is it we say, "What will be, will be"
only to plan, hope and dream?

Why do we hold ourselves to accomplishments,
admonish ourselves for failure
push ourselves to our outer limits
and trouble ourselves with worldly cares?

Why do we strive to achieve wants
which are not needed?
Could it be that living life's' course
is one of motion, a concerto of crescendos, a valley of lows
not attained through a depth of faith
but for wishes yet to be?

Trust

Our Lord surely know us
He knows our mind, our soul
He therefore always places us
in his wondrous control

For our my life were to be left
to us, and us alone
we would sink into the darkest depth
man has ever known.

But let us say, it is faith we have
faith in His control
it's a buttress for our weaknesses
bringing peace and joy to our soul.

It's a blessing so fulfilling, so complete
it is a treasure beyond compare
to know our Masters presence
is everlastingly there.

Faith, that when our time has come
to stand before our God
our Master, Lord, our Jesus
will take my hand and present me
before the throne unblemished
Loved

Jesus Loves the Little Children

(A Short Story)

How many hearts swelled with pride, as mine did that bright sunny June afternoon? Our daughter, bright, beautiful, and loving, was receiving her teaching credentials!   She would have such an impact on so many young lives, what a heartwarming thought that was. At one point in time, I did not feel, or could have ever imagined that this would be. The fact that prayers were answered is a testament to God's work in our lives.

It was to be a birth like millions of births occurring all over the world. With high expectations, Ron and I looked forward to starting a family. Three years following our marriage we had purchased a small home in anticipation. The baby's room was ready and waiting. We had the color scheme in yellows and greens for either a boy or girl. I could remember the day we laughed ourselves silly about what kind of toy to hang over the crib. We ended up with what Ron called a 'unisex ding-a-ling'. Now all we had to do was wait.

The day arrived, and as we hurried the twenty-four miles to the hospital, we spoke of our anticipation. We looked forward with eagerness to share our lives with this little one. You might say, we felt pretty proud and happy with ourselves. Everything we had planned and dreamed was coming to fruition, and we had made it all happen.

Day One

Arriving at the hospital, I was ushered into the labor room. My main concern was to be rid of the pain of contractions and to have a healthy baby. An expected short labor dragged itself into a full day and a half of tiresome, hurting pain. In and out of acute perception, clipped conversations – *"to weak, pain should lessen, not ready, I'll be back, we must do it now",* seemed to be swimming around me.

Day Two

I awoke rather groggily in my bed. Ron, with a frown on his brow, leaned over and kissed me. Even in my fuzzy realm, I felt the joy and anticipation of being a new mother. How I expressed this new status in my life to Ron. My anxiety was at an all time high as I wanted to find out if my baby was a boy or girl and if healthy and well. Ron responded that all was fine, but the concern now was that I get enough rest. He said that I had exhausted myself, and to go back to sleep. Hard as I tried, with the mid-afternoon shining brightly through the blinds, I could not hold my eyes open. With resignation, I succumbed to the warm blanket of quiet sleep.

Day Three

Somewhat disoriented, the cool morning nevertheless awoke me from my slumber, as the nurse in her crisp white uniform informed me not to sit up.

"Please do not sit up Mrs. Richards, you've had a spinal and the doctor wants you to be very still." "I'll be assisting you with your bath".

"How is my baby, is it a boy, a girl? Can I hold her?" Please, where is my husband?"

"Mrs. Richards, please try to relax, your husband will be in after your bath." "Your Pastor was in late last night and your little one was baptized." "We knew………."

My whole world collapsed! I shot up in bed, a whirlwind of thoughts, questions, emotions, interplaying with each other in my mind. Fright, pure, cutting, painful fright filled my mind, my lungs, my total being. My head was splitting, my throat constricted. *What had happened, why a baptism, where is my husband, why hadn't they let me see my baby??* Every muscle in my body seemed to be on fire. My baby, my child, my little life. She was everything I ever wanted, I needed that child.

Fate intervened as my doctor, husband and nurse walked in. With all love and compassion, it was explained my little girl's life was ebbing away. She was unable to breathe on her own; her lungs would not fight off the fluid. She had been born with a condition known as Erathmatosis Fetalis. As Doctor Kline spoke, my world came crashing down. How many times had I spoken to this little one as she occupied my womb. How many dreams did we talk about, first if she was a boy, then if she was a girl. How many songs did we sing together, plans we looked forward too. Dr continued speaking.

"There are a few more things we can try, but she is very weak."
"No, I want you to stay in bed, lay flat, rest,"

The nurse gave me a shot, I fell asleep. Waking up that evening seemed like an eternity. Ron had spent the better part of the day there, so gave me a lot more particulars, saying that I would be able to see her in the morning. I felt sick and could do no more than cry. Looking at Ron and seeing the helplessness in his eyes, I finally felt the warmth of sleep overtake me once more.

Day Four

I awoke knowing I would see my daughter. The nurse wheeled me into the area reserved for those infants in need. There she was, in an incubator, so tiny, so swollen, so many tubes. How my arms ached to hold her. How I marveled at her beautiful, beautiful face, those tiny hands, her little body, so small, and so vulnerable. I yearned to hold her for just a few minutes. I thought of how she would talk, how she would run to me, how she would call me "Mommy". I thought of all the wonderful beautiful moments I would be cheated out of. All the many dreams and joys so many young mothers dream of when first seeing that precious innocent soul that was so much a part of them. I hadn't even heard her voice! It wasn't fair! Where was God in all this? No, He would not cheat me out of this. Never! I don't need Him or anyone. We would make it on our own. *Get well, get well my little one, get well.*

How many times over and over I repeated this, as I gazed through glass windows at her weakness in life. *My little one, my daughter, so much a part of me. So tiny, so frail.* The old song, "Jesus Loves the Little Children", revolved in my mind as I gazed at her, my girl, mine.

"I'm sorry Mrs. Richards, but the doctor gave strict orders. You do want to get strong enough so you can get home".

It really wasn't a question, and as I was wheeled to my room, a sense of powerlessness overcame me. I wanted to pull the blankets over me and sink into oblivion.

Day Five

Brought up as an abused child, how I had longed for my own family. My own children. A husband to love and care for me. *Things would be different when I was grownup.* It just wasn't fair. I had lost my mother, lost my grandmother, and now was losing my daughter! When would it end. The day I met, then married Ron was joyful and was all the justification I needed that the meanness and sorrows in my life were gone for good. Gone were the sad, bad days. As long as I had my husband and children, I didn't need anything or anyone else. Now here it was again, fright and pain resurfacing, with a piercing rebirth of days gone by. I hated God at that moment. I hated the life he had given me. Just as I had felt I had wonderful things in my life, He was now pulling them away. Why? What had I ever done? Where was this loving God, this "Jesus Loves the Little Children" God. What about that little Angel in that incubator, she had never done anything wrong! Why would He take what is mine. What I formed and carried in my loins. He had nothing to do with it. She was <u>my</u> child.

As I sobbed uncontrollably in the darkness of that room, I prayed, *take me but not my daughter. Let her feel the love of her daddy. Let her feel the coolness of the breezes, the goodness of love and laughter in life. Let her feel the peace of your Spirit oh Lord. Take me, take my life, I give her back to you. Thank you for giving*

47

her to me for a few days. Forgive me, my doubts of you oh God. I hurt; I hurt so very, very much. Somehow in that strange realm of consciousness, of total helplessness, I felt a strange sense of tranquility. I felt assured that He would wrap his arms around this child, my child, and bless her all the days of her life. She, this little precious infant would grow to love and serve Him well. I thought of my husband, and with keen awareness, I thought of my God. Abba, Father, I slept.

Day Six

Ron greeted me as I opened my eyes. I had never seen him so utterly haggard. Doctor Kline was with him. Both men looked so forlorn, such heaviness permeated the room.

"Ann, you have to be brave", *what is this brave business and why doesn't he get to the point,* "We have tried everything possible to alleviate this problem to no avail." "She continues to lose ground." "Perhaps three, four hours." "It's now up to a much higher authority." "I would suggest that you and Ron prepare yourselves." "We won't give up, but there just isn't anything more we can do at this stage....."

For those of you who have heard words as this or similar pronouncements, my heart aches for you. Ron and I sat there, speechless. It was strange in an odd sort of way, I felt almost detached, yet somewhat bewildered. I remember saying to Ron that I felt we should pray. Ron looked at me and shook his head in bewilderment, unable to understand this request. I called my church and asked for a prayer chain. As we visited our little girl that day, I prayed, and yes I cried. When I bedded down for the night, I still had that feeling of being in less of a struggle, a sense that control had been taken out of our hands. Could it be the 'peace that surpasses all understanding?'

Day Seven

Much to my wonderment, I was awakened by a smiling nurse. In bounded the doctor and my husband.

"Mrs. Richards, what happened last night was just short of a miracle." "Your daughter seems to have improved, not out of the woods yet, nevertheless a significant improvement." "We want you to know this, but please don't get your hopes up too high; she still could go either way."

"Yes doctor, thank you, I understand fully."

I no longer had hope, for hope is something to come, but in its' place was a peace, a peace that was NOW. That peace had permeated my entire being. In place of hope was a blessed assurance.

How my heart swelled with love and pride that beautiful June afternoon. How I thanked Him that he had not abandoned me as I did Him, that night, so long ago.

Motherhood

Fifty years ago HE gifted to me – You,
why I pondered as I awoke
such a wonderful blessing
above all other things.

Was it so that I may relish
the indescribable love a child brings.
Is it that I may have the experience
of joy, pride, and tears, or even
frustration, patience, and expectation.

Perhaps it is that discernment
can be fostered and patience honed
or just perhaps, it would give me the ability to
share and teach our daily mundane tasks
while sharing the deeper values which stem from our faith.

Then again - it could be to teach me coping skills
with worrisome matters such as
Will she be happy, will she be well, will she make right
choices?
or how to be patient, how to encourage, how to pray and
how to be thankful for all life experiences, large and small.
All this to be learned from one brought into this world
through no choice of their own.

Now as I grow into my declining years,
I see a mature loving wife, mother and dutiful daughter
with strong faith endowed from above and within
well established in you, my girl – and I know, yes I know
the depth of Gods' loving favor bestowed on me that day.

Parenthood

*We have received a lifetime of blessings
through our children
because God is our Giver.*

*We have always had faith
in their new adventures
because God is our Encourager.*

*Our characters have deepened in His grace
and our joy excels in His gifts
because God is our Forgiver.*

*Were we not to see another day,
God has fulfilled us through
the joys of Parenthood along the way.*

Daughter

Daughter is such a beautiful word,
especially when it conveys
all the joys, tears and love
shown in so many, ways.

Like the deepest blue of skies,
or the brightest hues of sun
gentle sweet, full of life,
my daughter – you're the one.

Memories of laughter, peace, trust,
rendering my heart in bliss that's just
and so passes on from time to time,
a future that's yours. the present that's mine.

For we are here now, as woman and child
adding softness and beauty to this earth,
so when our time here has past,
our memories unto others will always last.

There the holiness of God's gift to man
will surface again and again
and that which is godly, decent, loving and true
will pass again, from me to you.

Reverie

See the campfires glowing, see the stars above
God is always with us, showing us his love,
if only we will listen, if only we would see
open up our eyes and ears to life's' eternity

Sounds will come as music
from the wind, the earth, the seas
Sight will come from beauty,
as the mountains, skies, trees

but you must listen with your heart
and seek with all your soul
for it is then that beauty abounds
and treasures shall enfold.

His perfect way and majestic balance
is for each and all of us,
for speaking through these glorious wonders
is God the great Creator — God, eternal love.

Beauty Subtleness

(A Muse)

Many times the subtlest beauties in our lives are unseen and unheard, but most certainly felt. As examples of this, let us muse over what is taking place in our very core, when being a part of such experiences. What is happening in that place of ours in which we yearn, perhaps even hunger for a sense of awe, amazement, even fulfillment.

What happens as you stand atop a high mountain, meadow awash with wild blueberries, the wind, cool and crisp caressing your face, tiny meadow flowers and mossy green tundra beneath your feet, surrounded by snow-capped mountains towering in the distance, proud and untouched?

What affects a person on being on ocean bottoms, observing the rays of sunshine permeating through the giant kelp beds as they sway with a rhythm of their own, their tall stalks reaching for the light above?

What is transpiring when observing a mother moose protecting her young, the intensity of her gaze, the spasmodic muscular movement of caution, the flight or fight determination - ready to be acted upon? Or what touches us when observing a creature as the Grizzly and her cubs, foraging in their own environment. The greatness of this magnificent animal, the fierceness and yet gentle, seemingly compassionate care of her young?

And, what do we really behold, as we lift our heads to view the spectacular sight of the Eagle, Osprey, the Pelican, as the breadth of their wingspan catch the unseen currents as they glide majestically beyond our touch on something we cannot see or hear?

Even to our own roots, what are we experiencing when holding an infant in our arms and feel the softness of those tiny little fingers and toes? Are we able to discern the unabashed look of trust in their eyes? Can we appreciate the reliance, the guilelessness, and dependency upon others for total survival? Are we truly aware of the totality of their innocence and the relationship we pose in their little lives?

What is the subtle beauty of all these experiences? Perhaps it is those feelings, unseen or unheard, yet stir us in our very core. This is what gives us light, what humbles us and draws us closer to our God. This subtlest, magnificent beauty. Only, only through Him, his grandeur, his touch, his creation does this come to full fruition.

Dances of the Seasons

Trees, lakes, streams and flowers,
crisp, cool evening air
birds, geese, ducks, hawks
are given to us to share.

Sharing the joys of spring sounds,
smells and senses aware
the birth of life abundant
speaks of living, loving care.

The heat of summer
the coolness of fall,
the cold serenest of winter
is here for us all.

The dances of the seasons
continues on and on
and yet these mortal lives of ours
have so short a time.

Belonging for one brief moment
to this world we claim, "Mine"
for when dust we are and
no more than thought
who will behold us as one begot,
as legends of time, men of worth
only One knows, our death, our rebirth.

Yellow Rose

Life would not
be as sweet
but for the Yellow Rose.

Its' Bud, like life itself
opens to full bloom
emitting its' fragrance
giving pleasure to those about.

Its' strength is in its' beauty
its' hope is in the
newness of life.

The joy it brings to others
as it shares its' lifespan
simple and unencumbered.

How much pleasure
how much sweetness
this rose
this beautiful Yellow Rose.

I Am

Remember Lord, Thy glorious works
the beauty, the abundance, the unbroken face
of undulant forest spread without rent or seam.
Thy lakes, mountains, marshes — tameless, unbetrayed,
all virgin of the spoiler, all inviolate.

I travel with softness, as a caress on ones' cheek.
No one sees from where I come or where I go,
but the leaves — their branches gently swaying
witness to my presence.
I am the Wind.

I run with zeal or pool myself to rest, unable to hobble my
course,
my pathways bringing into existence meadows, canyons
meandering through soils and rocks alike -
sculpturing a panorama along my path.
I Am the River.

My face is serene; my depth is ever changing
placid reflection of the skies above.
I sustain life not seen and give birth to that about me.
I invite all to share in my beauty, my bounty.
I am the Lake.

I tower over others, challenging wind, water, storm.
I reach for the skies, my face carved for others
to delight in its' awesomeness, or to conquer.
I kiss the stars, meet the moon, add pleasure to the rising
sun.
I am the Mountain.

The scents, the sights, the creation and recreations of lands
and waters, held in beauty undeflowered
where fear was not, nor hate.
Shall men now portend – in progresses' name, the rape
of this glorious, heavenly place?

Never Say Goodby

Good morning World – I awake.
The sun filters through the treetops
breathing life
on those of us below.

I stretch my weary bones
they once again become supple
and I am ready
for this new day.

Catch the wind
the power of the senses
cool mist in my face
I'm alive.

Hello life
listen to the leaves fall
hear the birds sing
feel the earth beneath my feet.

Soft cool meadows, rippling stream
I sense the space, the calm
which envelops me in reverie.
This is time, my moment.

The seasons in time pass
the fullness of growth peaks
giving itself up
for the new to begin once again.

I too, pass on
with my seasons and time,
Yet..........
Never Say Goodbye

Ripple of Life

No matter how small, how imperceptibly
one touches matter
it sends a ripple that resounds out to many
never alone, never unto ourselves
indeed, our thoughts and actions
reverberate unto others

It is impossible to touch a placid pool
without a rippling affect
this is proof of our existence,
life's course is the same.

Listen to the waves
resounding from others,
however at rest you may be,
it lays it's mark upon you.

Motion, whether yielding
toward peace or folly, is there
touching, changing, reflecting
creating and recreating.

It is its' own existence,
yielding itself
again and again, beginning to end
again and again.

Listening

(A Muse)

Listening, deep, quiet, intent listening – listening to the exclusion of all personal thought, allows one to gain worth in His sight. We are awed by His presence, glorified by His love as we seek His glory and receive His peace.

There are no cares or concerns that He cannot bear. There are no hurts that He can't heal. As we come to Him through his Son, there are no limits to His forgiveness.

We have no wisdom or strength, yet with our Lord, we are wise as Solomon, strong as Goliath. We are as precious as the most precious gemstone. He is our God and Creator. He is our Redeemer and our anchor.

If this is bestowed on us as a mortal, what is in store for us when we leave this mortal world? Will we have our hearts' desire, singing praises to your name? Will we draw a smile upon Thy lips? Will you lead us through fields of flowers and call us by name? Will we sense the joy beyond description of calling you Master? Will we no longer be stressed with the 'tug and pull', the 'ups and downs', the constant battles between heart and soul?

We look to our Soul as the great Comforter. Our heart sways back and forth as leaves in the wind. Our mind, a product of the existence around us, our Body a vessel of containment; yet we are not complete.

Perfection and holiness we seek through keeping steadfast and true to your name. Help us to know ourselves and what you would have us do with our lives. Guide us to help others in the knowledge that you are our resource.

Let us experience your healing hands, your grace, your love, your forgiveness. Let us validate these experiences so fully in this life, that our thoughts, our lips, our actions become reflections of the Living Word. Let our frailties become capable of gaining and giving strength to others. Let us rejoice in the Promises you made, but <u>first,</u> we must listen.

The Bustle of the Flock

So very busy as a Bee
are we far too busy to dwell on Thee
noting all the plans to come
all engrossed in what we've done.

So much to know and grasp
so much to learn and plan
so many places to go, to see
so many feeling besieging me.

So many prayers to pray
so many souls to save
so many calls to make
what or which will I do this day?

In your Name and for your sake,
glorious plans we strive to make
justifying thoughts and deeds
consumes our time on others' needs.

Busy busy as a Bee, stop and think collectively
are we just too busy to dwell on Thee
Stop.... Hush....Listen
Is that HE who's calling me?

Guidance

Take my hand Lord, show me
wonders of the Earth and
kindness of the soul,
know that I am but a pawn
among the strong, the bold.

Take my hand Lord, see me
through Thy loving eyes
see that all my needs are met
in life and paradise.

Take my hand, will me
to stand upon my own
with all the wisdom and the grace
that you've so lovingly sown.

Take my hand, heal me
of my wayward ways
May I always humbly pray
and thank You for each day.

Lord, take my hand and know me
and I will then know Thee
then all my thoughts, ways and deeds
will cause a change in me.

Preachers

They've elected to be a shepherd,
but do they know their flock?
they know that there are many
who would want to have them mocked.

Surely, to claim to be a shepherd,
one must always will to lead
seek out the frail, encourage the strong,
protect the weak, right the wrong.

A flock without a leader
is one in desperate need
for that flock must be shown the way
guided - where to feed.

We're in desperate need ourselves
so can't begin to guide
that flock through all their obstacles
life will cast alongside.

It then became so very clear
what they could do and when
the sheep became their flock once more
and began to follow again.

So pleased were they to cause this change,
until they turned around
aware it wasn't them they followed
but once again – twas HE

Lament

Oh Lord our God.…………..
We want to scale the highest peaks
and claim your name to all.
we yearn to shout their battle cry
that men may know your call.

We seek to preach unto the world
until each one has heard
how great Thou art, how good Thou art
then men may heed your word.

For we were born to do thy work
for You we'll change the world.
Men will know your grace, your love
We'll bring all to the Father, above.

Forgive us Lord
for it is not we that changes lives
nor we that have men honor Thee
but rather You, my Lord, through
Thy wondrous works – will cause a change in me.

Be Still

(A Muse)

The leaves turn their color but once, whether it is subtle or outlandishly evident, that change is never again repeated. Are we, too many times, too busy to notice?

Like the leaves, we change too. No matter how many times we feel that we are or have repeated a task we set out to accomplish, it is not a repeat in exact form. Something has been lost, gained, matured or different. Take time to look around you, see the rose and look again, there is change. See the individual, look again, change has occurred.

How is it, so frequently we hear the words, "I've already seen it"? The old adage of taking the time to smell those roses, can be a warning to those so involved with their conquests in life. So many times, the very act in seeking, seeking, seeking – becomes an entity in itself and it then becomes the conqueror and you the conquered.

In the pursuit of understanding or knowing others, as well as oneself and of appreciating life to its very fullest, "things" left undone may remain so for another time, another day. For what would be accomplished if to stop, if just for a moment to watch those leaves turn, or smell those roses.

What transpires in ones Being mentally, emotionally, intellectually, spiritually or even physically if for one brief moment we were to be still, just to observe the nature which surrounds us? What is happening when we look up at the awesomeness of the stars, shimmering so far above us on a cool crisp night. Consider feeling the rain or snow on our faces – what is transpiring within us when we see majestic peaks of the mountain tops, the meadows green, the rushing of rivers or the placid lake in various hues. What happens to be still enough to notice the oceans' relentless power or the quietness of a trickling stream?

Are we too busy, we haven't the time? Then you don't live, you don't truly live. You merely act, respond, leak out, give away, diminish your soul, your very nature, a part of your Being which changes , never to be recovered. For whether it's the positive or negative, the impact on your life is there for you to choose.

As for me, I will leave the mundane to be undone, if but for another time. For me, to take time to sit still and see the leaves turn, is to regenerate my soul. To take time to see, touch, feel, to observe and wonder at the beauty of that moment, that very minute, second, for it too will change, never to be recovered exactly as before. Those observations, taken but moments in my life, invigorate me, rejuvenate me, renew the spirit within me and fill me with more to give. Be still, be still.

Responsibility

Who knows ourselves,
our stand in life and
who accepts that part
which fails?

Who mocks our living,
our strife, our weaknesses,
strengths and ails -
Us – or our Being of Christendom.

For we must know that one
has passed our way.
It is He who gave his life
clearing the path for judgment day.

He carried the cross
separating chaff from wheat
that he may see us whole,
flawless, complete.

Creatures who before Him
stand proud and tall
through his Son,
our Christ, our all.

This, to us is the greatest measure
as we do his will and follow his way,
throughout our lives,
each and every day.

Growing Up

(A Short Story)

Two things you can say about November, its turkey month and it's cold. All I had to do was to stick my face out of my coverlet and watch the "smoke" rise from my mouth and nose. Of course, listening to Chet's' grumbling and carrying on was just as good. The walls that divided our bedroom were not all that thick and I could hear him grumbling. For a lanky twelve year old, he could chop wood about as fast as he could cuss. This meant I'd have to get out there and pick up the kindling, bringing it into the kitchen, so the old wood stove could start warming up the place.

Chet tolerated me, being a girl and all, because unlike Lettie, I'd help him with the wood and hold the pail when we went Crawdad fishing. Boy did he like to tease Lettie with those Crawdad when we'd get home.

This morning he was in a particular bad mood, yelling at me to get out of bed, which usually was a sign for me to holler back. This would, of course, bring a switch to both of us from mama or dad. But, this morning was special. I was not about to cause anything to spoil this day, so out of bed I hopped.

This being the first day of November meant Thanksgiving was just around the corner. This year was going to be different. After a lot of discussion, mostly on my part, we convinced Dad to let us have our own live turkey. Today was the day we would go to Mr. Jensen's' turkey farm to pick one out. Mr. Jensen was a stick of a man, with a craggy face and eyes of blue that would pierce your soul if you'd dare stir up his gobblers.

"Stirred up gobblers ain't good for the table", he'd say".

"Hey, Mr. Jensen"

"Hey to you too, Miss Annie. I've some jawing to do with your daddy. While we're about it, you go out there and choose one of them gobblers you want to take home".

Of course, he had to remind me not to "stir um up". The excitement within me was so huge, as I walked through that gobbler pen. He and Dad finally got through jawing, and Dad and I picked out the best gobbler in the bunch.

As soon as we got home, we penned up "Joe" next to the chickens so he wouldn't feel alone. Joe's the name I gave him for no other reason than he just looked like a "Joe". Jabbering all the way home, Dad said I might break my neck looking at Joe in the back of the pickup. I just wanted to be sure he wasn't too scared.

"Now don't go getting to friendly with that gobbler Annie. In a few weeks he'll be ready for the table". "Yes sir, nice and fat, and ready for the table".

During the next few weeks, it was all I could do to hurry up with my chores. These chores, of course, included feeding and watering Joe. In my spare time I'd walk around that pen, watching him run with that funny waddle of his and hear him gobble. Fact of the matter, was Joe and I became good friends and I'd decided to train him to come to me when I called. Chet said gobblers were the dumbest things on earth and that would never be. But, I knew I'd show him. Who knows, maybe I could train him to fetch. I was so excited for tomorrow to come. Even with Mamas' great fried chicken supper, I could barely eat.

Supper time was always a time when Lettie, Chet and I had to give the folks a rundown on what we had done and what was accomplished during our day. Listening to Lettie crow about how well she did in school, and what good things her teachers said about her was a prize bore. Chet's' accounts of having been provoked into a fracas of one sort or another, was a lot more interesting, but Mom and Pops always cut him short . I was so excited; I'd been squirming throughout supper for my turn to come. Being seven, and the youngest, I was always the last.

"Well Annie, how was your day today?" You've been squirming all through supper like you had ants in your pants".

"You'll never believe this", *this seemed to always be the introduction to a stupendous, momentous explanation, and therefore achieved the honor of having all within earshot hold their breaths for what it was they couldn't believe.* "I collard Joe today and he didn't run away." "We went out of the pen and he'd just gobble now and then." I think he's ready to start learning to come to me".

With that, Chet and Lettie burst into such an uproar of hee-hawing, not anywhere's as to how I thought they'd react. Mama shut them up while Dad shot them that, *you better settle down look.* Then he proceeded with telling me how our chickens brought us food and the like. It was the Lords way of providing the animals for our nourishment. I knew that, because many a time I'd help Chet chop off their heads, jumping quickly out of the way as they flopped headless to and fro. *What on earth did this have do with Joe?*

"You know Annie", my Dad continued, but not without throwing Chet and Lettie that look of *settle down there,* "how everything we have on our little farm is for us to eat and grow fit as a fiddle." "Why the smokehouse is filled with hams and sausages from our pigs." "Jessie, our cow provides us with warm milk and butter; our chickens give us eggs and the best fried chicken in the county". "Even our fruit trees and garden gives us about all else that is needed".

"I know those things already Daddy, but I want to tell you about me and Joe". "I really think he really, really knows me". With that, Dad gave a heavy sigh.

"You know what tomorrow is, don't you Annie?"

"Sure it's Thanksgiving. Uncle Ross, Aunt Eunice and my six cousins will be here for supper." "We're going to have turkey, ham and mamas' pickled apples for supper and pumpkin pie for dessert." *Another big sigh and that look again, to Chet and Lettie.*

"Tomorrow, early morning Annie, I want you to bring that gobbler...."

"Joe, Daddy, his name is Joe!"

"Alright it's Joe; bring Joe over to the back of the barn." "Perhaps it's time for you to learn a lesson". "Now Lettie, help your mother clear the table." "Annie, you get ready for bed. I'll be in shortly for prayers."

Never was I so happy. Dad must really be impressed with me training Joe. Why, I didn't even have to help clear the table!

Tomorrow, I'd show him how great Joe and I get along. Heck, maybe even my cousins would be here for that. Tomorrow was a big day.

Needless to say, it was a night of tossing and turning. Morning finally came and as the sun feebly tried to rise, cold or not, I jumped out of bed and readied myself for the day's events.

What a happy moment, Joe, my Joe, was to celebrate turkey day with us. Man, did I have a time catching him. He gobbled and ran his legs off. Finally having put a noose on him, much to his protest, I took him to my Dad, in the back of the barn, as he had asked me to do.

"Joe's a little nervous today, but I'll settle him down some." "Guess it's too early for him to be his best." "Hey Daddy, you've got your rubberalls on!" *Now, whenever mama wanted to fix her famous chicken dinners, Chet or Daddy would don their rubber boots and aprons. You see, in order to get them chickens heads off, you'd stretch its' neck out steppin on the head, and the other foot on the lower part of the legs. Then with one quick swoosh of the ax, off would come the head. Wearing them rubberalls kept one from getting splattered all over the place.*

"Oh, Annie, Dad sighed, what am I to do with you?" "Remember our talk at the supper table last night?"

I wouldn't call Dad a big man, like Mr. Roscoe on the next farm. Mr. Roscoe would bring Mama fresh buttermilk and beef. She'd always have fresh biscuits and cold fried chicken for him. It always amazed me how may biscuits he ate. To look at him, he could make three of my Dad. No, Daddy wasn't a big man like Mr. Roscoe, but he sure was tall and lanky like Chet. His big shoulders, arms and hands were suntanned from working out on the farm for years. But, his eyes are what I remembered the most. Large and soft brown, which turned a hazel, especially when he wore his Sunday "go to meeting" clothes. Those eyes captivated me as they did now.

"Look, Annie, the good Lord gave us the farm with these animals for a purpose." "Animals feed us, sustaining our health; they bring us money to help us keep our farms......."

"And sometimes, they make good pets Daddy," I interjected. With that, another long sigh.

83

"Hand me the gobbler Annie."

"His names Joe Daddy, Joe", *how many times did I have to say that!*

The look in my Dads eyes then told it all. Those wonderful soft brown eyes. The eyes that sparkled when he was proud of me, laughed when he had a surprise for me, and yes, were saddened when he hurt for me. That was those eyes now. Somehow, some-way, I knew I was learning the lesson he had talked about. My heart sank!

"Sure you want to stay Annie?"

"No Daddy."

As I walked away, I knew, I surely knew, and a little of my life changed.

Grandaughter

What do these aged eyes behold
as I look upon your face?
I see dreams, hopes, and eager anticipation
of worlds of experiences to come.

I see deep love, virtue, sweet honesty,
a diamond – radiant and bright,
character, strength, modesty,
a young woman – such delight.

A sprinkling of impishness, a large dose of joy,
a mind filled with inquiry -
challenging the very best,
never settling for less.

I see a true and humble spirit,
a credit to her God
a warm and caring person,
found guileless and loved.

You are the seed of my firstborn,
a child of my child
welcomed with such joy and care

Know my darling granddaughter,
that in my heart
You - will always be there.

Growing Up

I knew you would be a blessing
when you stubbornly arrived.
You were one little Angel
that filled my heart with pride.

You cooed and gurgled little ways
into your Nana's heart,
those sparkling eyes and sweet smile
they worked their wondrous part.

Then as a Toddler, you began to grow
your 'Carebears" all, placed in a row.
Counting them over, feeding them well
with tea and cookies and all that's swell.

We mustn't forget your 'Rainbow Brights'
you knew them all by name.
Your eyes would sparkle like a Gem
as you played your little games.

The dresses Nana made for you
And that dumb pink left-arm bear,
the doll house Papa built for you
we did, because we care.

Oh, don't forget our 'dress-up' games
with Nana's gowns and lace.
Scarf's tied prettily to your waist
and make-up on your face

Or those little 'Tea Parties'
in Nana's 'pretty room',
now look at you, all dressed up
sigh....the time flew by too soon.

Happy days, fun days, sad days too
alas, turn around, it was time for school.
Growing up, that's what it was
much too soon for Nana's rule.

The years passed swiftly,
the 'Teens' descend
heaven help me,
to this there's no end.

Horses, friends,
these interests are major,
My sweet little Princess
is now a Teenager.

Boys surely now
will take the scene
for you my dear,
are now Sixteen.

I really wish
this would not do
I'd rather wait
till your twenty-two.

But grow up you must
and so this I'll say,
You're in Gods' hands
in this I'll trust.

Children

Children as the flight of time
pass swiftly through our lives,
taking with them their dreams
and plans of future generations.

Conditioned with eternal hope,
love affirmed and reaffirmed,
drawing on resources of years past,
yielding to changes of the day.

Wisdom is a thoughtful act,
one of great discernment ,
wisdom knows no age or time,
holding true in righteousness.

Our children – may they know no hardships,
may their lives
be in concert with the goodness of life.

When does the child end, the adult begin ,
with silent subtlety - a breath
carrying itself with and as the wind
through years which pass too swiftly.

Might it be their joys are our sorrows,
that very act of joy used for learning,
growing , absorbing,
using their talents in their lifespan?

Soon – too soon, the day arrives
when they will use all of which was given them
making their own stand in life - Their life.

So why must hearts ache to know
their time too, has come,
for its then we say,
Go out, forage, learn, experience for yourselves"

Live your life
with gusto and compassion.
Share your dreams with those about you.
Be in tune with your innermost Being
and He who created you

As time, for you too my children – will pass all too swiftly.

Families

Some are large, some small —
colored in various hues
rich, poor, weak, strong, love or hate
are theirs to choose.

All same yet distinct in separate ways,
yielding to each other's needs
sharing in life's hopes and dreams
to reach an apotheosis.

For within each heart the mold has been set,
and though apart physically
we know the future lies within the past
as we create our families.

Each member being a part of the whole,
yet distinct, creating their own
each whole being a part of this legacy,
aptly choosing right from wrong.

These truths will surely diminish the growth,
of both the young and the old
unless prepared by this family
the family now in control.

Sisterhood

A sister is…..oh, such a pain,
a tattle-tale, or
laughing, sharing, fighting at times
such as, "what is yours" or "what is mine"

Childish scrapes, childish ways,
oh how they have passed
those childish days.

A sister is….Sweaters and skirts,
give or take, accusations of blouses torn
adoration of wiser ones
hopes and dreams of things to come.

How they have passed,
these many years
teenage laughs and teenage tears.

A sister is….Wife, Mother,
family of her own
concerns not shared
celebrations, joys and grief.

Busy sharing lives with others needs,
instilling values from deep in heart
to <u>her</u> children, <u>her</u> family
Is it now sisters part?

Then as we grow older,
and the years pass away
our families grown,
perhaps we're alone

Sisterhood, Allegiance,
Kinswoman, Friend
We find each other
once again.

Easing Ones' Way

(A Muse)

If to make life less difficult for others is one of our major purposes in this life, and if this aim is accomplished, what is the value to others and what is the impact to us, personally?

Does this translate into assuming the difficulties encountered, such as tasks, failures, illnesses or misfortunes unto ourselves? How would this stretch the physical or mental abilities of one? And what would this accomplish for easing the life of the recipient and the giver?

I dare say, should I attempt to sculpt, which to me is most difficult, and if one were to help me in this endeavor, how long would this ease last? Not very long, for if we are really to make life less difficult for others, empowering them to understand and accept their limits would be much more lasting. It is imperative to note that the acceptance and understanding of one's' limits does not mean hobbling or confinement.

It is enough to say acceptance and understanding brings about a clarity of attributes which allows us to have lesser constraints. The constraints being of misunderstanding those involved and the acceptance as to the kind of assistance needed.

It is then, the difficult pathways encountered are easier to address. Never-the-less, at times it seems so much easier and quicker, we think, to do something for others rather than encounter the errors, mishaps and inconveniences which may occur.

So if we are to live making life less difficult for others, let us do so by edifying and encouragement of their strengths and attributes.

It is then they will be "tuned in" to preparedness of the best possible way of addressing encounters in life which, at times can be quite perplexing. Ergo: my sculpting example, rather than helping me to sculpt, encouraging me in understanding and accepting my abilities and attributes would be far more lasting. It is that I apply this awareness to myself – you have then made my life less difficult.

The impact to a person from a physical, spiritual and emotional self-worth is then extended to the social aspect of their life. Making life better for others enriches ours. It would appear then, that as the individual is a part of the greater society, the society itself benefits as a whole.

Therefore, we must ask ourselves, how and which is the greater end of the process of easing ones' life – the encouragement and support or the "doing"?

Friendship

We've been given friends to fill our lives.
friends to share the good and bad,
to be there to comfort and encourage
throughout our mortal lives.

Friends can be defined in many ways,
from raucous to the sublime
friendship takes the "I" and "me"
and turns them into "us" and "we".

It takes fun and fairness to weave
these traits through me and you,
relying on each other for truth and compassion,
and instantly focuses on each others'
needs and reactions.

It negates failures through eyes of love
and gives self worth from the One above
It's distinct in the Deity we all share
having staying power, knowing our Lord is there.

Years fly by before we know the depth
of this concern
the love and warmth shared by this friend
is then easily discerned.

So to each and everyone of you,
I say again and again
May our Lord bless and guide you
and
thank you for being my Friend

Brown BEAR

Why do I give you "Brown Bear"
when already you've grown years old?
You think you've passed that stage of life
when you've outgrown your kiddies' toys.

I give you Brown Bear
to cheer you when you're sad.
I give you Brown Bear
to share those times you're glad.

To comfort and console you
when you're sick and feeling ill
I give you Brown Bear
when you're trying to find your way in life
through sheer strength of will.

I give you Brown Bear
to hug when someone reprimands
when you have that lonesome feeling
that no one understands.

I give you Brown Bear
to make you laugh, not cry
when you feel your failing
even as hard as you may try.

I give you Brown Bear
to remind you of the things you must do.
hold to your values
in the choices you pursue.

I give your Brown Bear
so that you will always know
how very much you're cherished
by a Nana who loves you so.

You and me

To be in partnership with you
in, feeling, loving, sharing
has shown me, in so many different ways
you are a man of caring.

Because what we do
does not determine who we are
but what we are
determines what we do, and
that, my husband dear
best describes the one I love -
that one I love, being you.

You are thoughtful
and therefore think of others.
You are loving
and therefore love.

You are committed
and therefore commit to others.
You are trusting
and therefore, I trust you.

There have been so many times
I've come up short and failed
and you were always there my love
making me feel special
telling me, "alls well".

Patience you have always shown
with my tempered ways
I will always love you dearly
throughout our waning days.

To share my life in Christ with me
makes you so very dear
my hearts' been full, my hearts' been glad
throughout these many years.

For you are more than just alive
you live, you love, you've soul
living, rather than just life itself
is just so beautiful.

Marriage

Marriage is made of fragile things,
a look, a promise,
a word, a ring
between a man and woman in love.

Frailties and strengths when shared
and bound by faith above,
will strengthen this partnership
with true and mature love.

Yet, should faith and honor as light, grow dim
or held in secret and never told,
this faith will then lack vitality
becoming joyless and cold.

Sharing is light and spreads its' warmth
reflecting prisms of joy and sheer delight,
such joy and happiness, fully complete
Marriage then, becomes so sweet.

It is within this union of two in one,
that strength and trust is grown
for it then focuses on each other,
rather than "to each his own".

It works at keeping criticisms
always at bay,
and allows Christs' workmanship
to have its' way.

Therefore, uplifting each other
with enthusiasm and grace,
sharing the peace instead of the sword
Thus
each is honored, and so is our Lord.

A New Bride

"You've come a long way baby"
that's what they say,
the struggles were worth it
to reach this big day.

Remembering the time
you were lovingly sown,
the years passed swiftly,
and now you're all grown.

You've plans for the future,
you and your own
creating a harbor of refuge,
a family, a home.

Savor this day, this moment
for it will never again pass
these are the memories your love
and you have begun to amass.

Your fortunes will tire,
and be spent in time,
but your memories, ah memories
will be given back in kind.

And so my darling daughter,
my first child, given from above,
I give you to your husband,
for him in Christ to love.

Love Letters

Love letters between
you and me
forever cherished they'll always be.

Plans and dreams
of things to come
hope and anticipation of when done.

Home, children, lifestyle, and more
where to live
City, Country, Suburb, Shore?

How and where will we work,
and careers to be
what's in store for you and me?

These pages of love letters
you'll find from the start
whether written or spoken,
bespeaks of my heart.

The years have now past
and the "plans" which were bold
will be read and savored,
once we are old.

Peace

(A Muse)

Peace – the absence of war or strife, no disappointments, void of grief. This is not the peace within us, nor is it a peace which is dependent on outside experiences or influences.

The peace within us is one of tranquility, sureness, harmony. It is able to withstand the onslaught of grief, pain, mockery or insolence. It is an assurance that is gained from Christ himself, and transcends all human defilement. It is an encourager, not a destroyer, a "lifter" of souls. It gives a sense of worth to ourselves and others.

Peace then cannot be defined as lack of strife, grief, hurt or pain; but rather that of assurance, offering the prevailing strength over and through these misfortunes. It enables us to triumph over our adversities in this life. It is independent of others. It is independent of circumstances. It is in each of us, actively engaged or laying dormant, always accessible and true. It is the summation of these qualities of Peace, in how we relate to others and our own life experiences.

People speak of "World Peace" as if it were an entity of its own; something which can be put on a shelf, to be taken down or set aside as one would dictate. Or more so, the argument that a peaceful people can be overcome, defenseless, conquered, when in actuality the inner Spirit which defines the quality of peace has sufficient strength when justified to withstand and defend in order to create a positive change. This is the relationship we should have with others. It is there in each of us, not defined as a culture, race or belief. It can be honed or neglected, you have that choice.

Peace – what has happened to this nation of ours, these people, blessed and given strength by our Lord. Have we strayed far enough that we now cannot distinguish our purpose for these mortal lives of ours? Has the "fruit" become so spoiled that the "vine" must be cut down in its entirety?

We proffer peace to others. We speak of the "Prince of Peace", yet through means of arrogant self- pomposity or unilateral decisions, we War, to bring about our definition of peace to others. Is this the peace we define ourselves with – is this the Peace our Christ defines?

First, we must understand that Peace is not a commodity, it is not something to "make" or something that "is". It is within each of us to share with others. Peace is action oriented, therefore involves the action of commitment to love, forgiveness, compassion and understanding. This is accomplished one to one. At times, it may be fraught with hostilities, pain or sacrifice, but will never erase the Peace that surpasses true understanding. This is Peace.

Understanding

There will be a time
for weeping, a time to cry
a season of life passes,
we say good-by.

There will be tears of sadness
and yes, tears of joy
for they are with their Master now,
now and evermore.

Perhaps you'll feel a numbness,
a rift so large and true,
surely a segment of your heart
feels ripped out of you.

But what a wonder and a blessing
that we claim from above,
knowing Their in His wonderful presence
and in the fullness of his love.

Have heart with these words,
knowing they live,
for peace and joy in their life now reigns
as they share in His radiance
no more strife nor pain.

Birthdays

It's through our tribulation
Strength arises
Through our trials besetting us
Patience develops

When we find ourselves in despair
Hope is being honed
and
hope never disappoints.

It's through these daily strife's in life
Love is perfected.
So as we age and though our eyes dim
we see a much clearer vision
of what lies within.

Remembering as our mortality
continues its' demise
our spiritualness continues to grow,
and it's in this celebration
of life

A celebration of age and growth
that to you I say,
meet it with joy and happiness
on this -
your Birthday.

Promises

Almighty God.........
Hold me as is seek your face,
give to me my rightful place
through your Son, my Christ I come,
the "I Am", the Holy one.
So perfect in his love and majesty

Father..........
As I humbly lift my face,
I so thank You for your grace,
even in this place of woe and strife
knowing of the promises you made
so long ago.

Abba..............
Let me share your holiness
that only Your grace can give
Bless me, keep me in your care,
let me know you're always there
keeping the promises you made so long ago.

Three Small Words

As I look at that Cross, its' timbers so bare
I ask, "What does it seem to say?"
It speaks of a life, so perfectly true
a life given for me and for you,
a willingness to take up the task

I'm filled with joy and filled with hope
contrition and sadness too
for so many times I fall so short
striving to know what to do
and yet, as I look at those timbers bare
I know – I know, my Master cares.

I look at that Cross, remembering those words
cried out so long ago,
they speak of Holiness and Grace –
for He would die to take my place.

Ah, such wretched pain, laid bare for all
yet yielding to the power above
so filled with peace and certainty
obeying with the ultimate love.

Those three small words, and it was complete
those three small words...."It is finished"

Thimble of Water

A thimble of water,
an ocean, a sea
how great is God's love
for you and for me?

The oceans have shores
whether dimly seen or not
its' coastline
defining its bounds

But God's love, which is limitless, wise,
deeper than deep, higher than high
diminishes this vastness
in depth and size.

So great is His love
so awesome indeed
That - is His love,
for you and for me.

Stormfront

How often we stop to observe
the stillness of nature
yet, that very stillness she projects
is but a façade.

High above, unseen with the naked eye
she boils and churns
the heavens with her might.

This quietness, this stillness,
is only the anticipation
of a time she will unfold
her wrath on the earth below.

The beauty of that moment
we cannot harness nor contain
for she opens her waters and lights the sky
with a vengeance of her own.

She loans us her winds and torrents,
for a time, yet to come again.
Our prideful eyes,
vainglory and conceit

cemented in our abilities
and power of control
are left to clean and salvage works
left in her wake.

See and hear us scurrying about,
attempting fortification against her wrath
powerless, helpless, for we cannot harness
nor control her will to ours.

She brings life as she destroys,
dictating the time, the place, the season.
Beautiful, magnificent, powerful
this nature, this storm.

Side by Side

Lord, you're always there
to pick up the pieces
You're always there
to wipe away our tears

You're always there
to lift and console me
You're always there.

You're within us when
we feel uplifted and feel at peace
You're within us when
we're awed with wonder.

Your Spirit bodes us well
You're within us
to clear the passage
giving us hope and comfort.

You're before us to absolve
our guilt and calm the water.
You're before us,
always ready to direct our path.

You're there throughout
our trails and errors
always listening to hear our call.

YOU ARE
Omniscient – Omnipotent – Omnipresent
therefore
You are our all in all.

The Gift

That God should love a soul as me
that He should will to save my life
lift me up — take my strife

His powerful sovereignty I recognize
with all contrition in my sourfull eyes
He is my glory — my very life.

He provides the only way to receive His light
redeeming us of our selfish ways
our unworthiness — our inner praise

He gave his Son to show the way,
the grandeur of this gift from above
reveals — HIS Power, Deity and Love.

The Spirit

When one develops their wings to fly
And chooses to go their way,
It is so simple to follow the world
and its' glamour which can lead astray.

Help is needed to stay the course
the Spirit will have the key
that it shall be said, that where thou goes
It shall always lead thee.

When one is at rest
and slumber takes hold
concerns of the world retreat,
cares then become so easily solved
all becomes tidy and neat.

Yet living goes on, the problems exist
and whether it is you or me,
Then it shall be said, that when thou sleeps
It shall always keep thee.

Slumber then passes and cares return
our mouths presume to parlay
with rhetorical lament the rights and wrongs
of things concluded that day.

It is then a glorious renewal takes place
and our eyes are receptive to see
that it shall be said, when thou awakes
It shall speak with thee.

Choices

(A Short Story)

Carolyn looked down at her five sleeping children. She and Mike had been married six years now. When they met, he had been caring for his three small children since his wife had died. They now had five, and this would make six. She thought of the child within her womb. The child that would mean yet another mouth to feed. Another child to clothe, worry about, care for, and yes, even at times to enjoy. With a heavy sigh, she proceeded to her small warm kitchen. She could always find solace there, in its' familiar smells and warmth. She loved getting up early in the morning before she had to begin busying herself with Mikes' breakfast and readying the children for the day.

Small yet cozy, Carolyn had dreamed many times of 'revamping' her kitchen. Perhaps, new pale yellow curtains with small Irises for the windows. She loved Irises. Of course the sink needed to be replaced. Scrub as she might, the chipped enamel seemed to mock her efforts, always remaining an ugly eyesore. Mike had to put in new faucets last year, when the old ones finally gave out. The linoleum was the big problem though. Any new 'gadgetry', as Mike called it, would have to wait until the floor was done. She sighed, so much to do and so little to do it with. They could hardly make ends meet as it was. One of these days she would have her bright, shiny new sink, her pale yellow curtains with the Irises on them, and perhaps even a new stove. Someday.

What happened? It was not supposed to be this way. All the wonderful intentions she and Mike had, seemed so many, many years ago. To an eighteen year old girl at the time, there was nothing but hopes, dreams, plans, and stars in her eyes. Those plans, now empty of fruition, were buried deep under the weight of the basic needs of life. The struggle to make a life, a good life, seemed so tangible at the time.

Mike was then, as he is now, a tall rugged man. Big powerful arms and shoulders, tanned from endless hours of outside endeavors. Those arms that always seemed to be able to cradle her, giving her strength, she so very much needed at the end of each day. Most of all were those eyes. She often thought of those hazel eyes. So many times they held a communication between them when no words were spoken. What happened? Was it the war, how proud he was when he enlisted. How dejected he was when they sent him home, "too many children", they had said. She could remember how they had talked about his enlisting far into the night. They knew they would miss each other, but with jobs being so hard to come by, they had decided it was for the best. Perhaps the family could benefit with more stability through this dreadful economy that now existed.

Mike was always what other folks called a 'go-getter'. He was struggling to get his contracting business going, feed a large family and meet payments. They just seemed to be always eking out a living, paycheck to paycheck. Now, they were to have another mouth to feed. Carolyn thought of the pride it must have cost him to have to end up washing windows for Hancock's downtown.

Hancock's was the largest store in Pine Oaks. She and Mike had talked about one day going in there and buying all they needed for the house. Sometimes, they would just look in the window and dream of better times. *Enough beds so the children didn't have to share. matching bedspreads and curtains for the girls' room. Vanities for all of them, instead of the fruit boxes covered with chintz, as they now had.* Now, here was her Mike washing windows for a pittance. How she hated to take him his lunch. She could feel, if not see, the condescending looks in the eyes of their more affluent neighbors. But then Mike would say they didn't pay the bills or feed his kids, and that he would pick up cow dung if he had too!

She thought about her circumstances in life, and the child within her womb. She thought of how she should tell Mike . What would his reaction be? Moreover, her current concern was, should she tell him at all. Dottie had said that at this early stage in a pregnancy, it would not be missed.

Dottie was her best friend, a confidant, someone she could always lean on, someone she could trust. She could count on her to offer various options and solutions to any given situation. She had in the past and she had now. Carolyn had felt so stressed and tired as she told Dottie of her pregnancy. The extra burden it would place on the family, the eking out a decent living for the kids they now had. True to her friends' method of reasoning, Dottie listed all the negative and positive issues Carolyn, herself had thought of prior to telling her. Aside from having a child to love, there was the unmistaken truth of cost, health, and burden.

Dottie first suggested Mrs. Cox, Carolyn was first appalled. The thought of consciously relieving oneself of a pregnancy was unheard of in her family. Sexual discussion of any sort was never addressed, let alone something like this! Why, had it not been for Mike and the gentleness of his nature, his determination to work himself to the bone, she doubted she would have the thoughts she had today. Her whole world of belief was that life itself was a sanctity, no matter what age or circumstance.

Carolyn was eighteen when she met Mike. He, on the other hand, was an 'older man', with three small children. Mike's wife had died giving birth to Annie. She had met Mike at a church potluck social. He had complimented her on her fried chicken. Then as now, those intense hazel eyes in that suntanned face mesmerized her. It was no surprise, following a whirlwind courtship, they were married. This was done much to the chagrin of both sets of parents.

Like most 'new marrieds', Davy coming along so soon had not been planned. Nevertheless, happiness abounded, knowing that they shared themselves through this child. The other three children accepted and willingly coddled Davy. War had broken out and the economy was failing. Times were hard, especially with four children. With Mike maintaining two jobs, one as a lineman for the railroad, the other as a window washer, they were able to stay the wolf from the door. In Carolyn's' eyes, that 'wolf' seemed to be getting closer and closer.

Carolyn often thought, had they stopped with Davy, things would have been less difficult. A miscarriage occurred shortly after, and then Valarie was born. By then, nothing had improved, and what little savings they had acquired had been used up on medical bills and Mike trying to get his contracting license. Why this was so important to him, Carolyn could never understand. Why be a building contractor when the economy was so bad, no one could afford to buy. It was a constant 'rob Peter to pay Paul' circumstance they found themselves in now. With children's medical bills mounting, Val having had meningitis and Annie's asthma attacks, it seemed as though they would never be able to get out of debt.

Now, here at thirty-four, Carolyn found herself with child. Dottie had told her that since she had two miscarriages, this pregnancy would be a big risk to mother and child. Carolyn's head ached as she again pondered what she should do. One thing she had been certain of, the choice was never what to do, but how to afford another child. She also thought of what would happen if Mike was again, left with so many children to raise, should something happen to her during childbirth.

Mrs. Cox had been introduced to Carolyn by Dottie and now had opened up another alternative. One that seemed to address and settle many of the financial concerns, at least, not add to those already in existence. Besides, hadn't Dr. Polk instructed her to be careful regarding another pregnancy. Why Jimmy, Mikes' eldest, was almost a man of his own, able to have children. This child would be so much younger than the rest. What would the neighbors think? Most important, how would she be able to pull this off without Mike's knowledge? What if something went wrong? She knew Mrs. Cox was discreet and Dottie was a true, trusted friend and would keep this to herself.

Everyone knew Mrs. Cox, at least all the women in a half mile radius. She never attended any church socials, was rarely seen out in her yard, but appeared friendly when spoken too. A somewhat demure creature, small in stature with pensive brown eyes and wispy brown hair that always seemed in disarray, although attempts of piling it in a bun were evident, she was nevertheless liked and respected.

It was rumored that she once was a physician's assistant. Sarah, Dottie's neighbor, said she was a retired registered nurse, and that her husband had died in the war. *Of course Sarah was the unofficial authority of all of Pine Oaks citizenry.* Carolyn remembered Mrs. Cox attending a meeting at Whittendon's Elementary once. That was when there was such an uproar regarding sex education for the fifth and sixth graders. She didn't talk much, except to acknowledge those who said hello to her, responding in a warm way. Carolyn invited her to the upcoming social, but she declined in such a sweet manner as not to hurt any feelings. The upshot was you could see her as a very compassionate and caring person. This was what Carolyn was pondering over, this warm sunny morning.

Carolyn again, thought of the five children sleeping. They had all gone through the normal childhood diseases. Valarie's hospitalization for meningitis had been terribly expensive and they were still paying on the bill. Dr. Polk said not to worry, but Carolyn could hardly wait to clear this debt. She remembered how the whole family celebrated when the news came that Val would be all right. They never regretted the cost one bit. Annie's bouts with asthma were a continuous worry and Leah's foot never did heal properly. This gave her a limp when she walked. Dr. Polk said this could be taken care of in a year or two. Two years had come and gone, and it still had to be done. Thank heavens the rest of the family was in good health.

Her thoughts strayed to Mrs. Cox. Just how healthy would she be if she continued this pregnancy? Would they be able to take care of Leah's foot? What if Annie had to be hospitalized again? The note on the house was due in two short months, pay it or lose the house! That was the reason Mike was working two jobs. What if one of the other children became ill, or fell, or broke a bone? She had a tendency to be anemic, what if something should happen. All the 'what ifs' kept coming up. Carolyn cringed, how was she to tell Mike, they were going to have <u>another</u> child.

A chill went through Carolyn as she thought of Mrs. Cox and realized the implication that this evoked. She thought of her health, mental and physical, and those of her children already here. She thought of the immeasurable joy they brought. She thought how hard it was to get out of this eking out existence. She felt so very tired, spent. She thought of Mike, Mrs. Cox.

Sighing from worry and fatigue, she picked up the phone. She heard it ring on the other end. She felt her mind was made up. Her palms were sweaty, her heart seemed as though it would beat until it burst. Even though she had convinced herself this was the best decision, she found her voice shaking as she answered the inquiry on the other end of the line.

"Mrs. Cox, th-this is Carolyn Applegate down the road from you."

"Yes Carolyn, your friend Dottie said you would be calling." *Her voice was soft, soothing, and Carolyn could envision this compassionate women.*

"I'm so glad you called, at times it's very difficult to make these kinds of decisions alone." "Would you like to make an appointment?"

Carolyn's voice was shaking so hard, she could hardly speak. It seemed every nerve in her body was in knots. The sanctity of life had been instilled in her through her faith, for as long as she could recall. No, it wasn't the age of the life, nor the circumstances of life. It was the life itself, precious, gifted and unique. She began to speak.

"Ah...." *She hesitated,* "Mrs. Cox I called..., I called........ to let you, *umm,* to let you know there is a church social coming up this Saturday, would you care to attend?"

As Carolyn put the receiver down, a sense of relaxation, peace, permeated her entire being. *You could almost say, 'a peace that surpassed all understanding'.*

Mike would be up soon. As the coffee perked, a smile came to Carolyn's lips. She had something special to tell him this morning. This warm wonderful morning.

Calvarys' Hill

You died for our sins, You died for our sins
You lifted us up O'Lord, for you died for our sins,
In this you said, Come in...Come in"
Oh Holy God, the great 'I Am', You died for our sins.

You conquered the depths, You lifted us up
You paid the price for a relationship above.
With a heart that's true, a gift so real
You paid the price on Calvarys' Hill

The grace, Your grace so freely given
You call our name, for you have risen.
We love you Lord, so profoundly true,
in wonderment, our very all is bound to You

The joy we have is awesome indeed
You fill our soul, our life, with all we need.
We strive to obey and serve you Lord,
not out of fear or reprise,

But only because we love you so
and know You are on our side.
So quite our heart and quiet our soul
so we may hear you say

"I know you well, Your heart is true,
this day and ever
I'll claim for you".

Resurrection

The reason for our celebration,
is the Act of Resurrection,
which yields a sense of security and love.

A love which can never be separated
whether past, present, future,
from below or above.

For it is God who is at work within us
the great Comforter – our Redeemer
clothing us in tenderness of heart.

He gives us humility, gentleness,
patience and is wise
so that development of mind - is that of Christ.

Now as we look to that Cross,
and see what was done
the blood shed , the wound healed
our joy is complete, our future sealed.

What love so great
to give ones' life
that when we die, we can look to meet
our loving Father - Holy and complete.

What an awesome wonder
that Cross
to know that this, our celebration
is the act of our Christ – this Resurrection.

Now – we are whole, so let it be
for He took up our cross on Calvary.
No words or act can ever diminish

Nuggets Of Gold

I've traveled far and had my say,
but you, my grandchild
will do it your way.

Lessons I've learned throughout my years,
Some have brought laughter
And some have brought tears.

Yet these few nuggets of gold
I'll share with you, and
perhaps they may help
to see you through.

Be kind to all who pass your way
their struggles and adversities
may keep them at bay.

Understand those who agree or differ from you
for know that in their personal way
they are passionate too.

Stay true to your beliefs and
don't compromise the truth
Just know that what you say
will bear out in what you do.

Accept personal responsibility
when you see you are wrong
humbling yourself this way
will make your character strong.

Initiate reconciliation when conflicts arise
don't stand on pride
for this only, and always tends to divide.

Keep hope in your life and
adhere to the truth
then you will be blessed in all that you do.

Happiness

(A Muse)

Am I happy? How do I know if I'm happy? How will I know if I'm happy? Should you have to ask yourself these questions – you're not. Happiness is not something which is found, but something which is.

It is within each of us and is released in sharing with others or giving to others. It is then, that it becomes tangible, for we see and recognize its' joy.

We must look deeply into ourselves. Happiness cannot be received, it can only be given, and when given, it awakens that part in each of us that is inherent, inborn. Seeking happiness from others is like floundering in a sea of madness, thrown to and fro, perpetually grasping at unseen and unattainable shadows.

Understanding ourselves, recognizing our wholeness and marveling at the complexities of who we are, how and what we are, then accepting the totality of our characteristics, brings about a gladness, a joy, that we are then able to impart to others – that's happiness.

Some pass on from this mortal life without ever understanding what happiness is. It is of such sadness to never understand that happiness is not an object or quest. It cannot be earned nor attained, for it lies within each ones' Spirit. It grows or diminishes accordingly as its' distribution to others is given. Life calls us to live, and living is hoping, dreaming, planning and giving. Yet what happens when frailties' beset us, when mind has been ravished and these dreams, hopes have fled beyond ones' grasp? Can it then be that an awareness of this giving, this love must be understood?

Happiness reminds me of Love. To be loved, you must give it away to others first. I speak not of love as a response to the physical or a response to a look, touch or experience of life. I speak of love which is emitted from our very core, a love which is unmeasured, without constraints or reason. This love is then unwavering and not dependent on words, thoughts or deeds of others. It is a love that is soft yet strong. A love tempered by our life's' experiences but exists despite those experiences. It is a love not quantified, a love which is absolute and being absolute, characterizes our very Being. This will then allow us to experience the peace which surpasses all understanding.

Peace which dwells in each of us, cultivating and honing the Agape Love is true happiness. This is happiness, which is boundless and never-ending, unrestricted and not dependent on others' thoughts or actions.

The love which yields happiness is always constructive, willing to edify others. It's given without restraint and returns to us, sculpting us so that our actions and words, to others expose this love in its' purest form. Happiness then can be said to be borne of love and when given away as love, returns – this is Happiness to treasure.

Foolishness

What foolishness it is to be
filled with such sentimentality
Emotions choking in my breast
bursting to be out and then at rest.
What foolishness is this?

What foolishness for tears to come
when thinking of my daughter, my son
and know that someday soon they'll be
adults – with their own families.
What foolishness is this?

What foolishness for hearts to swell
when seeing my love and knowing him well
The steady pace of toil and care
of love, grief, and happiness shared.
What foolishness is this?

What foolishness when seeing the rain
and feeling Gods' presence upon us again
with contrite heart, we still remain
his creation, His love, His private domain.
Ahhh
But it's not foolishness, my friend, It's LOVE

Son

I've often thought
If only the sights you could see
could be that of our Masters,
what beauty you would behold.

If only your hands were those
touched by the Lord,
what profound wonders
you would perform.

If only your heart could
do the talking,
there would never be
destructive words.

If only your soul
could hold your mind,
the accomplishments for good
of man would never end.

Oh, if your feet would
walk in the Masters
what mountains you would climb,
what oceans you could cross.

And now I see, as you have grown
and faced this world on your own,
You are – my son,
Fast becoming that man.

Strong honest and faithful,
compassionate loving and true,
I thank our Lord every minute of every day
that through His grace, He gave me you.

Grandson

Rocking horses, bouncing balls,
  fluffy huggie Teddy bears
    for he is a little one,
  no worries doubts or cares.

Bicycles, baseball gloves, skis, books,
  lunches and wooly bugs
    now, the child becomes a boy
  and yearns for friends and toys.

Grades, rooms, yards to clean,
  "Have I made the Soccer Team?"
    How he loves to boat and ski,
  so full of life and vitality.

Teenage years and teenage cares,
  feelings borne of self-esteem
    cars and girls
  now make the scene.

  "Oh No"

Are those whiskers on his chin?
Now dress and shaving kits are in.
Hold your breath to figure out,
for time has passed so swiftly now.

Then the boy becomes a man
and takes his place
with all the grace
of one who knows he can.

Son-In-Law

There's a person we know,
like no other
for he's special in our eyes, you see.
He loves and laughs
and cares for ours
he's very special to our family.

There are many blessings
in this life
such as health, wealth, comfort and joy
but, the greatest of all
is the care of our own, knowing
they are safe, secure, and not alone.

To have you as our daughters
Lover, protector, supporter and friend
a man of integrity and caring
is such an awesome blend.

So, with this verse,
we wish to say
how much your loved and respected
Son-in-Law — this day and everyday.

Grandparents

Our wonderful precious grandchildren,
as our sight fails and our health declines
we ask ourselves so many times
why are we here and what is our purpose?

We're surely not charged with clothing you
or seeing that your fed and well,
nor need we instruct or chide you
or attempt to be your Pal.

We don't help you with your homework
nor give you sage advice
perhaps a little reprimand in your lifetime
once or twice.

We do proclaim your innocents
care not to hear your vice,
encourage you in all you do
and always say, "That's nice".

Pet names we have for each of you
along with such memories they bring,
each in the small corners of our heart
that keeps beating as angels wings.

But know our loves' sustaining
no matter what you do
a Grandparents love is never measured
it's <u>always</u> deep and true.

Faith

While we travel this lifes' rocky road
Lest we forget how well our Lord knows us
our minds, our hearts, our soul
and though we may not always agree
we are in his wondrous control.

For if our lives were to be left
to us, and to us alone,
we would forever descend
into depths painfully known.

But let us say, it's through this faith we have
that it is affirmed, He is always in control.
It is a buttress for our weaknesses
bringing peace and joy to our soul.

It's a blessing that's so fulfilling
a treasure beyond compare
a life that is so completed
knowing our Master is there.

He picks up the broken pieces
of a life that has taken its' toll
so that when our time has come
we will stand before our God
humble, pure, loving and whole.

Memory

This is my memory – yes the memory of love
the memory of life itself, sweet, as the taste of honey
painfully wanting, painfully haunting.

Let me come and be one, nor do I dream
but live within the Godly essence of nature.
She beckons me to her breast, and it's then and only then
can I feel myself at rest.

Printed in the United States
By Bookmasters